leapfrog

Rhyme
Time

Giraffe's
Good Game

First published in 2008 by
Franklin Watts
338 Euston Road
London
NW1 3BH

Franklin Watts Australia
Level 17/207 Kent Street
Sydney
NSW 2000

A CIP catalogue record for this book is available
from the British Library.

ISBN 978 0 7496 7944 6 (hbk)
ISBN 978 0 7496 7956 9 (pbk)

Series Editor: Jackie Hamley
Series Advisor: Dr Barrie Wade
Series Designer: Peter Scoulding

Printed in China

Franklin Watts is a division of
Hachette Children's Books,
an Hachette Livre UK company.

leapfrog

Rhyme Time

Giraffe's Good Game

by Margaret Nash

Illustrated by Bruno Robert

W
FRANKLIN WATTS
LONDON·SYDNEY

Giraffe was fed up.
His legs were too long.

He thought he was clumsy
and did everything wrong.

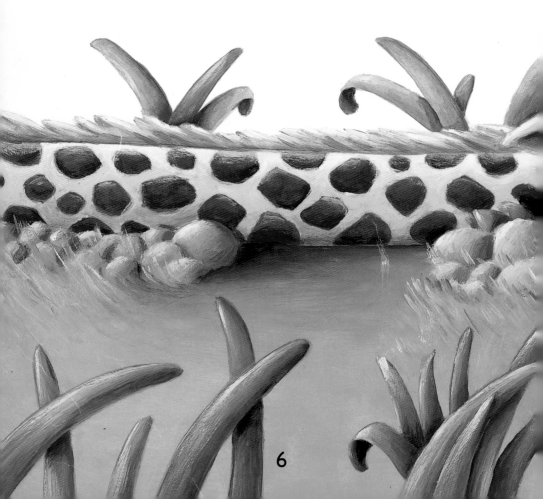

The others had fun
playing games every day.

But when Giraffe
joined in, he got
in the way.

"Why don't you try this?"
his friend Monkey said,

as he rolled over and
stood on his head.

Giraffe did his best,
but he got in a muddle.

His legs tangled up
and he fell in a puddle.

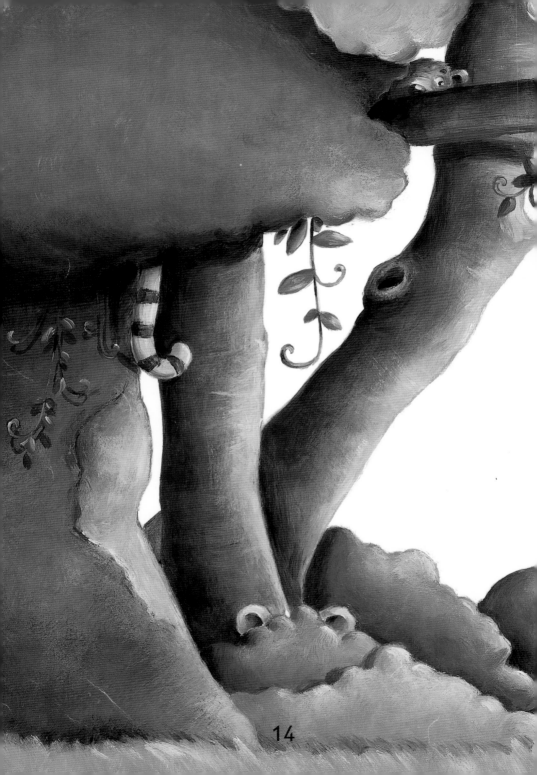

They tried

Hide and Seek ...

15

... but that was no good.

He got found too quickly
wherever he stood!

They played
Hunt the Pebble ...

19

... but Giraffe was too tall.
His head was too high up
to see things so small.

21

"Let's climb trees!"
the babies all cried.
They loved to climb up,
and look down from the sky.

And only Giraffe
was able to see
that the babies climbed
too high up in the tree.

The scared babies cried,
"Help! We're stuck
up here!"

Then clever Giraffe
had a brilliant idea.

"Slide down my long neck!"
Giraffe quickly said.
The babies jumped down,
one by one, on his head.

"Whee!" said the babies.
"This is good fun!"
And that's how Giraffe's
Good Game was begun!

Leapfrog Rhyme Time has been specially designed to fit the requirements of the Literacy Framework. It offers real books for beginner readers by top authors and illustrators. There are 27 Leapfrog Rhyme Time stories to choose from:

RHYME TIME

Mr Spotty's Potty
ISBN 978 0 7496 3831 3

Eight Enormous Elephants
ISBN 978 0 7496 4634 9

Freddie's Fears
ISBN 978 0 7496 4382 9

Squeaky Clean
ISBN 978 0 7496 6805 1

Craig's Crocodile
ISBN 978 0 7496 6806 8

Felicity Floss: Tooth Fairy
ISBN 978 0 7496 6807 5

Captain Cool
ISBN 978 0 7496 6808 2

Monster Cake
ISBN 978 0 7496 6809 9

The Super Trolley Ride
ISBN 978 0 7496 6810 5

The Royal Jumble Sale
ISBN 978 0 7496 6811 2

But, Mum!
ISBN 978 0 7496 6812 9

Dan's Gran's Goat
ISBN 978 0 7496 6814 3

Lighthouse Mouse
ISBN 978 0 7496 6815 0

Big Bad Bart
ISBN 978 0 7496 6816 7

Ron's Race
ISBN 978 0 7496 6817 4

Woolly the Bully
ISBN 978 0 7496 7098 6*
ISBN 978 0 7496 7790 9

Boris the Spider
ISBN 978 0 7496 7099 3*
ISBN 978 0 7496 7791 6

Miss Polly's Seaside Brolly
ISBN 978 0 7496 7100 6*
ISBN 978 0 7496 7792 3

Juggling Joe
ISBN 978 0 7496 7103 7*
ISBN 978 0 7496 7795 4

What a Frog!
ISBN 978 0 7496 7102 0*
ISBN 978 0 7496 7794 7

The Lonely Pirate
ISBN 978 0 7496 7101 3*
ISBN 978 0 7496 7793 0

I Wish!
ISBN 978 0 7496 7940 8*
ISBN 978 0 7496 7952 1

Raindrop Bill
ISBN 978 0 7496 7941 5*
ISBN 978 0 7496 7953 8

Sir Otto
ISBN 978 0 7496 7942 2*
ISBN 978 0 7496 7954 5

Queen Rosie
ISBN 978 0 7496 7943 9*
ISBN 978 0 7496 7955 2

Giraffe's Good Game
ISBN 978 0 7496 7944 6*
ISBN 978 0 7496 7956 9

Miss Lupin's Motorbike
ISBN 978 0 7496 7945 3*
ISBN 978 0 7496 7957 6

Look out for Leapfrog

FAIRY TALES

Cinderella
ISBN 978 0 7496 4228 0

The Three Little Pigs
ISBN 978 0 7496 4227 3

Jack and the Beanstalk
ISBN 978 0 7496 4229 7

The Three Billy Goats Gruff
ISBN 978 0 7496 4226 6

Goldilocks and the Three Bears
ISBN 978 0 7496 4225 9

Little Red Riding Hood
ISBN 978 0 7496 4224 2

Rapunzel
ISBN 978 0 7496 6159 5

Snow White
ISBN 978 0 7496 6161 8

The Emperor's New Clothes
ISBN 978 0 7496 6163 2

The Pied Piper of Hamelin
ISBN 978 0 7496 6164 9

Hansel and Gretel
ISBN 978 0 7496 6162 5

The Sleeping Beauty
ISBN 978 0 7496 6160 1

Rumpelstiltskin
ISBN 978 0 7496 6165 6

The Ugly Duckling
ISBN 978 0 7496 6166 3

Puss in Boots
ISBN 978 0 7496 6167 0

The Frog Prince
ISBN 978 0 7496 6168 7

The Princess and the Pea
ISBN 978 0 7496 6169 4

Dick Whittington
ISBN 978 0 7496 6170 0

The Elves and the Shoemaker
ISBN 978 0 7496 6581 4

The Little Match Girl
ISBN 978 0 7496 6582 1

The Little Mermaid
ISBN 978 0 7496 6583 8

The Little Red Hen
ISBN 978 0 7496 6585 2

The Nightingale
ISBN 978 0 7496 6586 9

Thumbelina
ISBN 978 0 7496 6587 6

Other Leapfrog titles also available.

Pet to School Day

First published 2005
Evans Brothers Limited
2A Portman Mansions
Chiltern St
London W1U 6NR

Text copyright © Hilary Robinson 2005
© in the illustrations Tim Archbold 2005

British Library Cataloguing in Publication Data

Robinson, Hilary, 1962-
        Pet to school day. - (Zig zags)
        1. Children's stories - Pictorial works
        I. Title
        823.9'14 [J]

ISBN 0 237 52848 7

Printed in China by WKT Company Limited

Series Editor: Nick Turpin
Design: Robert Walster
Production: Jenny Mulvanny
Series Consultant: Gill Matthews

ZIG ZAG

Pet to School Day

by Hilary Robinson
illustrated by Tim Archbold

Evans

"Today is pet day,"
said Mr Spink.

"Where's your pet, sir?"

"At home. He's too wild."

"Is he a bull?"

9

"Is he an elephant?"

11

"No," said Mr Spink.
"My pet is a...

…dinosaur!"

14

"Have you had him for
thousands of years?"

"I caught him on Sunday.
He wears a red collar, eats
trees and drinks from the bath."

"Where can you catch dinosaurs?"
"In a dinosaur park."

"How?"
"With a dinosaur net,"
replied Mr Spink.

21

"Can anyone do that?"

"Only with a permit," said
Mr Spink.
"When you catch a dinosaur
you get a badge like mine."

"How can you get a permit?"
asked James.

"You have to show that you are a brave dinosaur warrior," said Mr Spink.

"You're not!"

"How do you know I'm not?" asked Mr Spink.

"Because you're scared of
spiders and," said James,
"to prove it, this is…

29

Max!"

Why not try reading another ZigZag book?

Dinosaur Planet   ISBN 0 237 52793 6
by David Orme and Fabiano Fiorin

Tall Tilly   ISBN 0 237 52794 4
by Jillian Powell and Tim Archbold

Batty Betty's Spells   ISBN 0 237 52795 2
by Hilary Robinson and Belinda Worsley

The Thirsty Moose   ISBN 0 237 52792 8
by David Orme and Mike Gordon

The Clumsy Cow   ISBN 0 237 52790 1
by Julia Moffatt and Lisa Williams

Open Wide!   ISBN 0 237 52791 X
by Julia Moffatt and Anni Axworthy

Too Small   ISBN 0 237 52777 4
by Kay Woodward and Deborah van de Leijgraaf

I Wish I Was An Alien   ISBN 0 237 52776 6
by Vivian French and Lisa Williams

The Disappearing Cheese   ISBN 0 237 52775 8
by Paul Harrison and Ruth Rivers

Terry the Flying Turtle   ISBN 0 237 52774 X
by Anna Wilson and Mike Gordon

Pet To School Day   ISBN 0 237 52773 1
by Hilary Robinson and Tim Archbold

The Cat in the Coat   ISBN 0 237 52772 3
by Vivian French and Alison Bartlett

32